The Stolen Goblet

D0048131

Collect all the Charmseekers —

The Queen's Bracelet
The Silver Pool
The Dragon's Revenge
A Tale of Two Sisters
The Fragile Force
The Stolen Goblet

from August 2011
The Magic Crystals
Secret Treasure

from October 2011
Star Island
Moonlight and Mermaids

from 2012
The Mirror of Deception
Zorgan and the Gorsemen
The Last Portal

www.charmseekers.co.uk

The Stolen Goblet

Georgie Adams

Illustrated by Gwen Millward

Orion
Children's Books

First published in Great Britain in 2008
by Orion Children's Books
Reissued 2011 by Orion Children's Books
a division of the Orion Publishing Group Ltd
Orion House
5 Upper St Martin's Lane
London WC2H 9EA
An Hachette Livre UK Company

1 3 5 7 9 8 6 4 2

A catalogue record for this book is
available from the British Library.

ISBN 978 1 4440 0294 2

Printed and bound in the UK by
CPI Mackays, Chatham ME5 8TD

www.orionbooks.co.uk
www.charmseekers.co.uk

For Sally and Connie, with love.

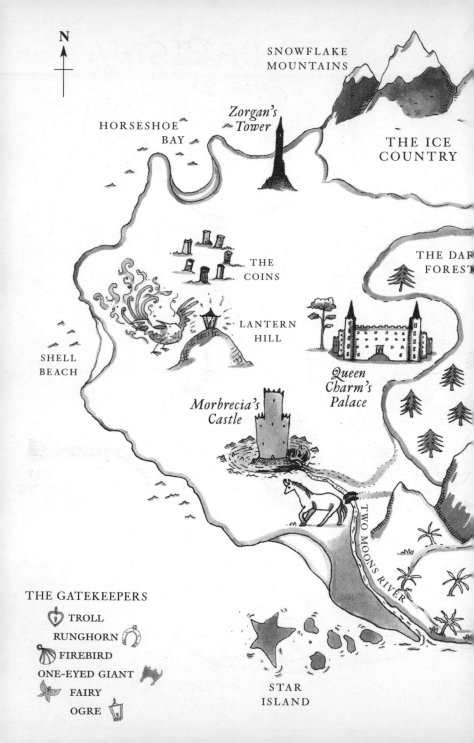

The Thirteen Charms of Karisma

When Charm became queen of Karisma, the wise and beautiful Silversmith made her a precious gift. It was a bracelet. On it were fastened thirteen silver amulets, which the Silversmith called 'charms', in honour of the new queen.

It was part of Karisma law. Whenever there was a new ruler the Silversmith made a special gift, to help them care for the world they had inherited. And this time it was a bracelet. She told Queen Charm it was magical because the charms held the power to control the forces of nature and keep everything in balance. She must take the greatest care of them. As long as she, and she alone, had possession of the charms all would be well.

And so it was, until the bracelet was stolen by a spider, and fell into the hands of Zorgan, the magician. Then there was chaos!

One

"Oooo! What will Queen Charm say?" gasped Ozina, the queen's maid. "Dork's in trouble."

She was taking Charm her breakfast in bed. On the breakfast tray was the morning paper, and a headline splashed across the front page had caught Ozina's eye.

THE CHRONICLE
First with the news around Karisma!

AN EXCLUSIVE REPORT FROM
OUR ROYAL
CORRESPONDENT

QUEEN'S GUARD

IN CHARMSEEKERS MIX-UP

AN INCIDENT took place recently near Butterfly Bay in which Officer Dork, one of the queen's guards, attempted to arrest Sesame Brown and her friends. Dork found Sesame, an Outworlder, in possession of one of thirteen silver charms from the queen's missing bracelet.

Officer Dork was unavailable for comment, but it is believed he mistakenly apprehended Sesame Brown, also known as a Charmseeker, on advice from Princess Morbrecia that Sesame was stealing the charms and taking them from Karisma.

The gatekeeper at Butterfly Bay, a fairy called Pogg, confirmed that four Charmseekers had arrived and left through her gate. She identified them as Sesame Brown, Maddy Webb, Gemma Green and Liz Robinson.

"Phew!" said Ozina, when she'd finished reading. "Her Majesty won't like this." She neatly folded the paper and tapped on the bedroom door.

"Come in," called Charm.

Ozina found the queen wide-awake and sitting up in bed. She'd had a restless night. Ever since her charm bracelet had been stolen, things had been going wrong: the Silver Pool had almost dried up, unseasonably bad weather had caused floods, crops were ruined, and strong winds had prevented Golden Ringlet butterflies migrating north to pollinate the clover. How she longed to have her bracelet back, to set things right!

4

"Good morning, Your Majesty," said Ozina, placing the tray on the bedspread. "Tissam,* toast and, er . . . your paper."

"Thank you," said Charm. She was always pleased to see Ozina, who'd been her loyal maid for many years. While Ozina busied herself drawing back the curtains, Charm opened *The Chronicle* . . .

"Hushish!"** she exclaimed. She jabbed the front page with her finger. "I wonder who's given this story to the paper?"

* *
* **Tissam** – a tea made from the dried leaves of the tissam shrub
** **Hushish** – a word used to express dismay

"I haven't a clue, ma'am," said Ozina truthfully. For once even *she* was behind with the gossip!

Charm took a sip of tissam to calm herself.

"Things are bad enough without having to worry about eavesdroppers!" she said.

The Silversmith was shocked to read the headlines, too.

Poor Sesame! she thought, as she rushed to the palace to see Charm. My suspicions about Morbrecia were right! I knew she'd be involved in this, and not for the good of Karisma either.

She found Charm pacing the floor, looking upset.

"Morbrecia deliberately misled Dork about Sesame," said the Silversmith. "She told him some twisted story and convinced him Sesame was a thief!"

"I'm afraid so," said Charm. "Luckily, Sesame has managed to find some of the charms before my sister. But what happens if Morbrecia finds the others first?"

"Sesame has your bracelet and five charms," the Silversmith reminded her.

"Of course!" said Charm. "Sesame has the heart, horseshoe, shell, cat and butterfly. Is it *possible* she'll find the others, too?"

"Sesame, and maybe her friends, will return

soon," the Silversmith reassured her. "They're all Charmseekers, but Sesame is special. She has the rare gift of the Seeker. Even if Morbrecia *and* Zorgan try to make trouble, Sesame won't give up, no matter what!"

* * *

Returning to her workshop, the Silversmith looks at the thirteen magic candles; eight glowing beacons remain burning. She closes her eyes, snaps her fingers *click!* And at once she's in a trance.

She holds Sesame in her thoughts, conjures her face and the jewellery box she placed in the Outworld, so many moons ago. Ah, yes! There's the bracelet and the five magical charms, safe in her Charmseeker's care. Softly she begins to sing *The Song of Charms*, and her sweet voice echoes across time and space, like a thousand tinkling bells . . .

Thirteen charms on a silver band,
United hold our world in hand.
May this gift for good Queen Charm,
Keep Karisma safe from harm.
One and all, beware the day
Charms and bracelet break away.
Together they must always stay . . .

Two

Sesame's room was unusually tidy. It had taken her all afternoon to sort through the jumble of tops, jeans, jodhpurs, trainers, pony magazines, CDs, books, bags, pens (just *some* of the stuff that littered her bedroom floor!) and put everything away. She'd strung twinkling fairy lights around the walls and was busy blowing up silver-coloured balloons.

"Maddy, Gemma and Liz are coming for a sleepover tonight," she told her teddy, Alfie, who knew about all her friends. "I can't wait."

She blew up another balloon and added it to the pile by her feet.

"Oh, Pins!" wailed Sesame. To her surprise, an aura of tiny silvery stars hovered over the burst balloon for a split-second – then was gone.

How weird, she thought, and was putting the balloon aside, when her dad tapped on her door and came in.

"Everything okay?" Nic asked, as Pins scampered through his legs.

"Hi, Dad," said Sesame. She shooed Chips away before *he* could cause any trouble then noticed her dad was wearing a new shirt and tie. "Coooool. Going somewhere? *Meeting* someone?"

"Uh-huh. Maybe," said Nic. He had a twinkle in his eye and was being deliberately vague.

"D-a-d," drawled Sesame, giving him one of her 'I-won't-give-up-until-you-tell-me' looks, although she had an inkling she knew what was coming.

Nic smiled. He noticed Sesame was wearing her favourite necklace – a silver chain and locket with tiny pictures of him and Poppy (Sesame's mum) inside. Although Poppy had died when she was a baby, Nic wondered how his daughter might react to him 'seeing' someone else.

"I'm meeting . . . Jodie," he said. "I've booked a table at The Lantern House. It's a new Chinese restaurant. I hope you don't mind?"

Sesame rolled her eyes.

"Of course I don't mind, Dad!" she said, and gave him a hug. "Love you."

Just then the doorbell rang.

"That'll be Maddy, Gemma and Liz," she said. "Maddy's mum is bringing them. Oh, I haven't done my hair. I'm *WAY* not ready!"

Sesame grabbed a hair-band then raced downstairs, sweeping back her long brown hair as she went. By the time she'd reached the bottom her grandmother, Lossy, was already opening the front door. She'd been making pizzas and her hands were covered in flour.

"Here we all are!" called Mrs Webb, half-hidden behind three girls, loaded up with sleeping bags, pillows and overnight paraphernalia.

"Come in, come in," said Lossy cheerfully, above a noisy chorus of greetings between Sesame and her friends. Everyone was talking at once. It was pandemonium! When Nic joined them, he held up his hands in mock surrender:

"Help! A house full of girls. I'm out of here."

Lossy laughed.

"Yes, off you go," she said. "I'm in charge tonight."

"Good luck," said Mrs Webb.

Sesame kissed her dad goodbye.

"Have a nice time with Jodie," she whispered.

"Thanks," said Nic, touched by her warmth. "You have fun too."

✳ ✳ ✳
✳

They spent the evening watching DVDs, munching pizzas, cream cheese dips (Sesame's speciality) and drinking fruit smoothies. When Lossy's friend popped in for a chat, the girls went upstairs to chill out.

"Mega makeover time!" said Gemma, wielding a hairbrush and straighteners. "Who's first?"

They all tried out fantastic new hairstyles with sparkly hairclips, ribbons and styling gel, until Liz remembered she'd brought some face packs.

"Gorgeous glowing skin in just fifteen minutes!" she read from a sachet of Exotic Papaya and Pomegranate. "There's enough for all of us."

So the girls slapped on the creamy mixture and waited for it to work.

"Aaaggghhh! I look like a monster," said Maddy, holding up a mirror.

They all got the giggles and didn't stop, until they'd washed their faces clean.

Later, while they sat around listening to *Crystal Chix' Latest Hits*, Sesame caught sight of her jewellery box. It glistened under the fairy lights, as if to attract her attention.

"Look," she said, opening the lid, to show the others. "Queen Charm's bracelet and five silver charms."

"Oh, they're lovely!" said Liz. She'd been with Sesame when they'd found the butterfly charm in a huge spider web.

Sesame picked up the exquisite little cat.

"I found this one in a horrid bird's nest," she said.

"After I'd fallen down a cliff," added Maddy.

"And I'd pulled you up," said Gemma.

Liz sighed.

"There's *so* much I don't know," she said. "You *said* you'd tell me. Remember?"

"Yes," said Sesame. "Well, it all started that day I was waiting for Maddy outside **Tip Tops** . . ."

✳ ✳
✳ ✳

By the time she'd finished her amazing story it was past ten o'clock.

"Thanks," said Liz happily. "I think I know all about the Charmseekers now."

"We should have a secret sign," Maddy suggested.

"Yeah," agreed Gemma. "Something that only Charmseekers know."

"How about this?" said Sesame. She curled her thumbs and forefingers to make the letters 'C' and 'S'.

"Brill!" chorused the others.

The Charmseekers were trying out their new hand sign, when Lossy's head appeared round the door.

"Bedtime," she said. "It's getting very late."

Sesame yawned and that set them all off.

"Okay, Gran," she said.

"I'll pop back and say goodnight," Lossy promised, and she left them to get ready for bed.

After sleeping bags and pillows had been arranged on the floor, the girls put on their pyjamas. Crystal Chix were singing one of Sesame's favourite tracks; she grabbed Alfie and twirled him round and round.

"My Prince Charming . . ." she sang, and Maddy, Gemma and Liz joined in, too:

My Prince Charming,

He's no fairy tale.

Real cool and disarming,

Gonna keep right on his trail.

Prince Charming!

Don't ever go away.

Together we must stay . . .

But as Sesame sang the last line, she felt a tingle at the nape of her neck. She touched her locket and it felt warm. Then she heard a strange voice singing:

Together they must always stay!

She was sure it wasn't the CD. This soft, sweet sound was eerily different.

"What's up, Ses?" asked Maddy.

Sesame didn't answer, because what happened next took them all by surprise. The balloon (the one Pins

had popped earlier)
blew itself up into a
huge, silvery bubble.

It grew bigger
and bigger, until
somehow Sesame,
Maddy, Gemma and
Liz found themselves
standing *inside* it!

Sesame's tummy flipped a
somersault. She prickled with
excitement as she wondered what lay in
store. All the while she could hear the voice
echoing inside her head – like a thousand tinkling
bells –

Together they must always stay . . .

Suddenly the enormous bubble gave a lurch and
lifted off the floor.

"Ooooooooo!"

went the girls, clutching each other to steady
themselves.

Slowly, the magical sphere spun round and drifted through Sesame's bedroom wall. Up, up, up they went, higher and higher into the moonlit sky. Soon the Charmseekers were sailing across the starry heavens, on their way to the magical world of Karisma.

Three

News of Sesame's attempted arrest spread fast, like drakons* devouring a crop of clover. Everyone in Karisma knew about Queen Charm's stolen bracelet, and took great interest in stories about the missing charms. However, Princess Morbrecia was none too pleased to read about herself in *THE CHRONICLE* that morning.

"Dork!" she exclaimed, flinging the newspaper across the room.

* *

* **Drakon** – a large, fire-breathing insect

23

"That doofer* told my sister everything! She'll *know* I'm after the charms."

The paper landed near a chair where Morbrecia's doll, Elmo, sat watching her every movement. Morbrecia picked her up, remembering how Zorgan had given her the doll on her sixth birthday. He had been Court Magician in those days, and the young princess thought he was wonderful.

"How things have changed!" she told Elmo. "If it hadn't been for that balam** magician, I would still have the bracelet. To think, I could have ruled Karisma! I'm the eldest sister. I *should* be queen, not Charm."

Even so, Morbrecia was sorry she'd quarrelled with Zorgan. He could have been useful to her. She looked out of the window. So far her efforts to recover the charms had been unsuccessful, and the gribblers*** (who were supposed to be helping) had failed her. Bitterly she thought of Sesame, who'd taken *five* charms to the Outworld! She *had* to be stopped, but how?

Morbrecia sighed.

* *

*Doofer — idiot of the first order, brainless

**Balam — cursed, an angry exclamation

***Gribblers — extremely unpleasant goblin-like creatures with yellow teeth and bad breath

"I must admit I could do with Zorgan's help," she confided in Elmo. "He *is* a very powerful magician— "

Just then a violent gust of wind blew the window open. The sudden force of it knocked Morbrecia back and sent Elmo flying. The doll landed on the floor with a *thump!* She blinked, and blinked again.

Morbrecia stared at her, fascinated. She had long suspected Elmo possessed magical powers; in the past there *had* been a few unfortunate 'incidents', for which she was sure Elmo was responsible. But what was this?

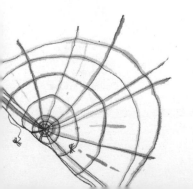

Elmo's lips were moving. Words came tumbling from her mouth, speaking in a voice — not her own — but one Morbrecia recognised at once. Zorgan!

"Let us leave the past behind.
Trust me, princess,
I have a scheme –
To win the charms and make you queen!
Then Queen Morbrecia
You shall be.
Now, let's be rid of S - e - s - a - m - e !"

Morbrecia gasped.

"Quisto!* Zorgan heard what I told you," she said to Elmo. "But I wonder why he wants to help me?"

Morbrecia wasn't a fool. She didn't really trust the magician, but she was intrigued. Hm! she thought. Supposing Zorgan *could* deal with Sesame? What if together we could recover all the charms? It *may* be to my advantage to patch up our quarrel . . .

* * * * * * * * * * * * * * * * * * *
* Quisto! — an exclamation of surprise

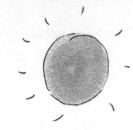

Four

Dawn broke over Karisma in a blaze of colour. The sky was turning bright pink as the bubble glided low over the Dark Forest, and set the Charmseekers down with a *bump!* They had landed on a marshy area known as 'the swamps'. The walls of the bubble seemed to melt away, as the girls walked out into a fine, silvery mist.

Slup! Squelch!

"Yuk!" cried Sesame. She'd stepped straight into a boggy patch and her slippers had filled with water.

"We're in our pyjamas!" exclaimed Maddy, squelching along behind.

"Brr! I'm cold," said Gemma, pulling her thin top over her bottom.

"I hope we don't meet anybody," said Liz. "I'd be *SO* embarrassed!"

The girls looked around to see if anyone was about. Ahead they saw a wooden bridge, which crossed a narrow canal;

they also noticed a rowing boat moored nearby, bobbing up and down on the water. They had begun to think they were alone, when someone shouted at them:

"STOP!"

This command was followed by a resounding

hiccup!

The girls stopped dead in their tracks. Blocking their way stood a monstrous ogre who appeared to be swinging a club. But, as the ugly creature came striding towards them, they saw (to their immense relief) that the 'club' was a giant gherkin, and that the ogre was taking great bites out of it. He hiccupped after every bite.

"Who – **hic** – are you?" he bellowed.

Bravely Sesame stepped forward, her feet squelching horribly inside her slippers.

"I'm Sesame Brown," she said. "And these are my friends Maddy, Gemma and Liz."

"Oooo," said the ogre. He'd read all about the girls in his morning newspaper. He grinned at Sesame from ear to ear, while crunching the warty gherkin.

"You're those, er, thingameblobs. Oojamaflips. Watchamecallits—"

"Charmseekers?" suggested Sesame.

"That's it!" he said. "I'm Bogal – **hic** – Gatekeeper Six. Have you come to look for Her Majesty's missing hoo-hars?"

Maddy, Gemma and Liz got a fit of the giggles, so Sesame said quickly:

"Charms! Yes, Sesame Brown will track them down! We must start looking for them straightaway."

Bogal waved a large, hairy hand towards the rowing boat.

"Take my oojamacallit," he said. "Follow the thingamy. It'll take you to the edge of the whatsit. But beware the thingameflips. They're having a hoo-ha tonight."

"R-i-g-h-t," said Maddy, struggling to make sense of what he was saying.

"Thanks!" the girls chorused, and quickly clambered aboard Bogal's boat.

"What time do we have to be back?" asked Liz, taking up one of the oars.

Bogal held up a gong and struck it with what remained of the gherkin.

BONG!

"You must return before the watchamaflip bongs six."

In his Star Room, Zorgan looked through his powerful telescope and marvelled at the brilliance of the early morning skies. When an enormous silvery bubble drifted into view, he adjusted the lens and could just make out the shapes of four girls inside. He tracked the strange sphere until it landed, and watched the girls step out . . .

"Blatz!"* he cried. "Those Charmseekers are back!"

Nearby, his pixie puppets, Nix and Dina, stood alert, awaiting their master's commands. Their cold, steely eyes glinted in eager anticipation. First, Zorgan barked orders at Nix:

"Follow the Charmseekers. Find out where they go and report to me. Sesame mustn't get away with another charm!"

"Yes, Master!" said Nix, and she flew off to carry out her mission.

"Now for Morbrecia . . ." Zorgan thought aloud. "I *think* I've persuaded her we should join forces, to recover the charms. What a fool I was to throw them away! They burned me so." He rubbed the scar on his wrist. "If *only* the fabulous bracelet had worked for me. Pah! That vermy** Silversmith made very sure it wouldn't. But *if* Morbrecia could wear the bracelet, I'd empower the charms with Dark Magic and they would be under

* *
* Blatz – a really angry exclamation
** Vermy – a miserable worm

MY control. Morbrecia must become queen to possess the bracelet but I'd be the *real* power behind the throne!"

He took up pen and parchment and wrote a secret message to Morbrecia. Although he could communicate through Elmo, Morbrecia didn't possess magical powers to respond in the same way.

He rolled up the parchment and handed it to Dina.

"Take this to Morbrecia," he said. "I must have her reply immediately!"

Zorgan's
SECRET
MESSAGE

Can you decipher the
magician's code and read
his secret message to
Morbrecia? Each symbol
represents a letter.

Zorgan's Secret Code

A – wizard's hat
B – drakon
C – web
D – dark cloud
E – spider
F – magic thorns
G – snake
H – frog
I – tower
J – wolf
K – skreel
L – mask
M – spell book

N – ghost
O – crystal ball
P – cauldron
Q – gribbler
R – pixie
S – rat
T – lightning
U – bat
V – volcano
W – skull
X – crossbones
Y – wand
Z – goblet

Five

The girls took it in turns to row in pairs. Liz and Gemma went first. After a hazardous start — they bumped into the canal bank (once) and went slowly round in circles (twice) — they eventually managed to steer the boat on a straight course. Soon they were skimming along and making good progress. The early morning sun rose high in the sky, warming the Charmseekers in their flimsy nightclothes. The girls chatted as they went along.

"I bet Bogal thought we were crazy," said Maddy, idly trailing her finger in the water. "I mean, look at us. In our pyjamas!"

"Anyway, it was cool of him to lend us his boat," said Liz, pulling hard on her oar.

"Mm," said Sesame. "I wonder what he meant by the thingameflips?"

"No idea," said Gemma. "But whatever they are, they're having a hoo-ha tonight!"

Everyone laughed and spent the next few minutes trying to guess what could be going on and where it might be happening. Later, when it was Sesame and Maddy's turn to row, Liz pointed ahead to some trees. As they drew near, Sesame thought the gigantic trees with blue-spotted leaves looked familiar.

"I climbed one the first time I came to Karisma," she told the others. "I was picking leaves for Fig—"

"—An *adorable* baby tunganora!"* added Maddy, who'd met him too.

* *

* Tunganora — a small ape-like animal with long, pink shaggy hair, which feeds on the blue-spotted leaves of the tuntree

"So we must be on the edge of the Dark Forest," continued Sesame, and a little shiver ran down her spine. "I rescued Hob from some horrid gribblers in there."

"Hob is Fig's mum, right?" said Liz. "I remember you telling us at your sleepover. It seems ages ago."

Sesame nodded and for a moment she thought of home. It was strange thinking about her room, a million miles away . . .

Crunch! The boat ran aground and Sesame was jolted back to Karisma. As they jumped ashore and tied up the boat, they heard the sound of the gong:

Sesame, Maddy, Gemma and Liz set off with Sesame leading the way along a narrow path. The girls felt a strange sense of foreboding hanging over the forest, like a dark cloud. The towering trees seemed to close in on them threateningly. Branches rustled. Twigs snapped. They were sure the trees were whispering about them!

38

"Totally weird," said Liz, seeing a face in one twisted trunk. "It's as if they're alive."

"Yeah," agreed Gemma, she could feel goose-bumps on her arms. "I'm sure they're watching us."

"I think they're sad about something," said Sesame quietly. She sensed a mood of deep unhappiness within them. "I wonder what—"

A chilly breeze brushed their cheeks and they saw an eerie spectre glide across their path. It was followed by another and another – countless forest phantoms, moaning and sighing. These were the Tree Spirits.

"Oooh!" said Maddy, clutching Sesame's arm. "I'm scared."

"Come on," said Sesame. She was determined not to let anything put them off their quest. "The sooner we find a charm and get out of here, the better!"

They moved faster through the forest than before, and as they went along Sesame reminded everyone which charms they were looking for.

"There's a coin, star, moon, lantern, snowflake, cloverleaf, dolphin and a key still missing," she said.

Just then a flash of light caught her eye; something sharp and bright was glinting in a bush. Excitedly she parted the branches, hoping to find a charm, but to her disappointment there was nothing but leaves and twigs.

"Found something?" asked Maddy.

"No—" said Sesame. "Ssh! Listen."

They heard the frantic whirring of wings and, to their surprise, Nix flew off through the trees, like a deadly arrow. Maddy groaned.

"She must be spying on us like last time."

"Come on," said Sesame. We *must* find a charm before she comes back!"

It was not a promising start. The Charmseekers made their way deeper into the Dark Forest. Every now and then they caught sight of the ghostly Tree Spirits drifting through the forest, like wisps of mist. Soon, too, they were aware of the unmistakable smell of rotting fish. It was a sure sign there were gribblers about! Every now and then they heard loud *CRACKS*, followed by the sound of falling trees. They had paused to decide where to go next, when two pink, furry animals came leaping through the branches.

It was Hob and Fig!

"Sesame! Maddy!" cried the tunganoras, landing at their feet. Fig was so excited, he ran round and round *whooping*. Meanwhile Hob was looking inquisitively at Gemma and Liz, who she hadn't met before.

"Meet my friends," said Sesame, and quickly introduced them. Then a serious expression came over Hob's face.

"Thank goodness you've come," she said. "Bad things are happening. Gribbler trouble!"

"Tell us," said Sesame.

"We'll help if we can," said Maddy.

Gemma and Liz nodded enthusiastically.

"Well, it's the Feast of the Stolen Goblet tonight," said Hob. "Gribblers are coming from all over the forest to celebrate—"

"Ah," said Gemma. "That's what Bogal was warning us about. The thingameflips hoo-ha."

The girls nodded and Hob went on:

"They drink potion from a goblet—"

"The goblet that was *supposed* to have been stolen from Agapogo," said Sesame. "The one in the legend."*

* The Legend of the Silver Pool — Do you remember the story? You'll find it in Book Two: *The Silver Pool*

"Yes," said Hob. "Gribblers think potion makes them strong, you see. They're making buckets and buckets of the stuff. That's bad enough, but they've captured some of my friends to make it! They've been making them work for days."

The girls were horrified to hear Hob's story. They looked at each other, and gave their secret sign.

"We're Charmseekers, right?" said Sesame. "But first we must rescue the tunganoras!"

Away in the distance they heard the gong:

Six

Morbrecia had agreed to meet Zorgan at a secret rendezvous at sunset. She wrapped herself in a black velvet cloak with the hood well up. I don't want anyone to see me talking to that slitey* magician! she thought.

"So, Morbrecia, we meet again. I regret our silly quarrel. But we must make up for lost time! From now on we must work as one, to possess those missing charms."

"Yes, yes, but Sesame Brown is very good at finding them. How can we stop her?"

* *
* **Slitey** – sly or untrustworthy

"I have an idea. It is a little difficult to explain, but I'll try. I believe the Silversmith has a bond with Sesame, which must be broken. The Silversmith has found a way to 'communicate' with her chosen Seeker, perhaps through something precious . . . something that belongs to Sesame, which is very important to her.

"Sesame Brown is determined to find all the charms and return them to your sister. BUT if I were to hold this special thing, I could curse it. Then Sesame would be under my spell and bring US all the charms!"

"I've got one of her shoes. She lost it when I was chasing her on Agapogo Day, around here. Would that do?"

"Er, it's not *quite* what I had in mind. A shoe might be useful for sticking pins in, to give Sesame a headache.

45

No, there must be something else. A favourite doll? Or perhaps a piece of jewellery?"

"Well, I've seen Sesame wearing a pretty silver necklace and locket—"

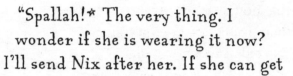

"Spallah!* The very thing. I wonder if she is wearing it now? I'll send Nix after her. If she can get it, we shall soon have Sesame in our power!"

* *
✫ Spallah – excellent! a triumphant expression

Seven

Hob and Fig took the Charmseekers to the edge of a clearing in the forest. She told them that the gribblers had cut down many trees, stripping their branches bare of blue-spotted leaves, to make potion. And where each tree had fallen, its eerie spirit appeared – like the ones the girls had seen earlier. The spectres were shaking their ghostly limbs in anger and wailing:

"Enough! Enough! Too many of us have fallen! Cut down in our prime."

"The Tree Spirits are angry with the gribblers for cutting them down," explained Hob. "They moan and sigh day and night."

"They sound so sad," said Maddy. "It makes me want to cry."

"Me too," said Gemma. "I didn't know trees had feelings."

Already the sun was lowering in the sky; at this time of year the days on Karisma seemed very short, and Sesame reckoned it would soon be dark.

They stopped by a fallen tree and Hob indicated for them to crouch behind it; from here they could watch what was going on. The girls gasped. It was a ghastly sight and the stench of rotting fish was overpowering. A chain gang of tunganoras were fetching leaves and tipping them into buckets of liquid. Others were being made to chop down trees and everywhere there were gribblers, shouting at the tunganoras to work faster. The biggest gribbler was stirring a massive cauldron of foul-smelling potion bubbling over a fire, and singing:

"Never mind the pong,
Never mind the weather.
Potion makes you strong,
Potion makes you clever.
Stir it with a stick,
Mix it till it's thick.
Take the cup and slurp it up –
Potion makes you SICK!"

"Who's that?" asked Gemma. She thought she'd seen him, the last time they were in Karisma.

"Varg," said Fig. "He's the worst!"

"Where's the goblet?" whispered Sesame, wishing she had a handkerchief to cover her nose. She was almost choking on the fishy pong.

"There," said Hob. She pointed to a shiny silver cup perched on a tree stump and guarded by two gribblers. "That's Gorz and Bod," she added.

Sesame wondered what to do. Soon a wild plan was forming in her head and she turned to Maddy, Gemma and Liz.

"If I could *steal* the goblet," she whispered, "the gribblers would come after me, right? It might give you enough time to free Hob's friends?"

"Ses!" protested Maddy. "If the gribblers catch you, they'll boil you in that bucket!"

"It *might* work . . ." said Liz slowly. "Maybe we should split up. Gemma and I could distract their attention, make spooky noises, that kind of stuff—"

"—And I'll go with Ses," said Maddy firmly. She wasn't happy about the risk her best friend was about to take, but at least she'd be there to help.

After they'd talked for a while longer about their rescue plan, Sesame smiled and said:

"Okay. Let's go!"

"Setfair,"* said Hob and Fig.

The girls went their separate ways and, as they went, they heard the sound of the gong echoing through the forest:

Bong Bong Bong Bong

* *

* Setfair – goodbye and good luck

Eight

The Feast of the Stolen Goblet had begun. A mass of fat, foul-smelling gribblers, their hideous bodies covered in blobby warts, had gathered round the fire. Thick green goo dribbled from their fangs as they pushed and shoved each other to guzzle potion from the goblet. Varg, Gorz and Bod were in charge of the ceremony, frequently passing the goblet between themselves, while smaller (though no less

smelly) gribblers carrying lanterns, were rowdily singing the potion song:

"Never mind the pong,
Never mind the weather . . ."

Nearby sat a pathetic group of exhausted tunganoras, roped to a tree. From their hiding place Sesame and Maddy watched the proceedings, while listening out for Gemma and Liz. They had agreed that spooky noises would be the signal for them all to spring into action!

Meanwhile, Gemma and Liz had been creeping through the undergrowth, keeping well out of sight of the gribblers. In the dark, neither of them noticed the layer of criss-crossed branches lying across their path.

SNIP, SNAP. CRICK, CRACK!

The sound of snapping sticks was quickly followed by surprised yells, as the girls fell into a – PIT.

"Aaaaargh!"

screamed Gemma.

"Woooaaar!"

shrieked Liz.

They had fallen into one of the many traps set by the gribblers, for catching unsuspecting tunganoras.

"Oh, no!" moaned Gemma. "I can't see a thing."

"Ouch!" yelped Liz. "I've trodden on something. My poor foot."

"Ow–Ooooooo!"

Sesame and Maddy heard their cries.

"There!" said Maddy. "That's our signal from Liz and Gemma."

"I'm going for the goblet!" said Sesame.

"I'm right behind you," said Maddy. "Go!"

They sprinted across the clearing, two shadowy figures silhouetted in the firelight. Just as Varg was about to take another swig of potion from the goblet, Sesame sprang, taking the gribbler completely by surprise. She snatched the silver goblet from his greasy, grimy fingers, spilling the revolting potion over his feet. Then she RAN.

"Ssheshame Brown!" bawled the furious Varg, when he saw who it was. He yelled at the crowd of gribblers, spraying them with a shower of slime. "After her! Shee mushn't get away!"

Meanwhile Maddy, who had been busy untying the tunganoras and setting them free, looked up and saw that the forest clearing was suddenly full of Tree Spirits, shaking their branches and moaning:

"WHOOOOO! WHOOOOOO! WHOOOOO! WHOOOOOO!

The gribblers shall pay.
It is time. It is time!"

They had come to take their revenge. Their gnarled and knobbly features twisted grotesquely, as they cursed the gribblers for cutting them down, and for treating the tunganoras so cruelly.

For a fleeting moment Varg, Gorz and Bod were rooted to the spot, unable to believe their eyes. For once, Varg was speechless and stood there dribbling.

57

"We've been drinking too much potion," said Gorz.

"I'll never touch another drop!" said Bod.

Then the cowardly gribblers dropped their lanterns and fled in all directions – any thought of pursuing Sesame forgotten.

Soon afterwards, Sesame came running up to Maddy, panting. She was still holding the goblet.

"What happened?" she said. "I nearly got trampled to death! The gribblers went racing by me, as if they'd seen a ghost."

Maddy grinned.

"Loads of them, actually," she said. "The Tree Spirits came and scared them off." But when Sesame looked around, there was no sign of them anywhere.

"Where are Liz and Gemma?" she asked.

"No idea," said Maddy, realising she had been too busy with the tunganoras to notice they weren't there.

Next thing they knew, Hob was running towards them, frantically waving her arms.

"Come quickly," she said. "I've found your friends!"

It was pitch black and freezing cold at the bottom of the pit. Gemma and Liz huddled together to keep warm, while they waited to be rescued. So it was a great relief when, at last, they saw Sesame and Maddy smiling down at them from above.

Hob, Fig and the rescued tunganoras had picked up lanterns, left by the fleeing gribblers. They shone their lamps into the pit, so Sesame and Maddy could see to help Gemma and Liz climb out. As Liz was waiting to be hauled up, she felt something dig into her foot again. And now that it was caught in the lamplight, it sparkled silvery bright.

"Hey!" cried Sesame, reaching down to grab Liz's hand. "What's that by your foot?"

When Liz stooped to pick it up, she squealed with excitement.

"It's a charm!" she said, holding up a tiny silver lantern, for them all to see. "A beautiful silver lantern."

And as the two moons rose in the night sky, they heard the sound of the gong:

Bong
Bong
Bong
Bong
Bong

Nine

"That was five bongs on the watchamaflip!" said Liz, remembering Bogal's words. "We must hurry."

Sesame and the others had been looking at the little lantern, turning the charm this way and that, admiring every detail. It even had a tiny light. Sesame knew she must keep the precious charm safe, until she could place it in her jewellery box. There were no pockets in her pyjamas, so she clasped it tightly in her fist.

Everyone said their goodbyes and the tunganoras thanked the girls over and over again for their help.

"I hope the gribblers stay away for a long time," said Maddy. "Those Tree Spirits really gave them a scare."

Sesame handed over the silver goblet to Hob for safekeeping.

"If this goblet really *was* stolen from Agapogo," said Sesame, "perhaps one day the dragon should have it back."

"You're right," said Hob. "I'll find a good place to hide it, and the gribblers need never know!"

The Charmseekers ran back through the forest, to where they had moored the boat. Sesame grabbed one oar and Maddy the other, while Gemma untied the rope.

"It took us ages to get here," said Liz, sounding anxious. "I hope we'll get to the gate in time."

As Sesame and Maddy began to row, a gentle breeze got up and pushed the boat along. Gemma and Liz gasped and pointed to the banks. They were lined with the ghostly forms of Tree Spirits, waving their branches to bid the Charmseekers farewell.

"WHOOOOO! WHOOOOOO!

The friendly spirits sent the boat skimming along so fast that Sesame and Maddy shipped their oars, and let the wind take them all the way to gate. Bogal was waiting for them, banging his gong.

BONG, BONG!

"Hurry," shouted the gatekeeper.

BONG!

"Where's the balloon?" shouted Gemma.

"Just head for the swamp," yelled Sesame, running full tilt towards it.

"Quick!" yelled Maddy. "We'll just make it."

BONG!

Sesame had almost reached the swamp when, out of nowhere, came the angry Z-z-z-z-z-z-z of whirring wings. It was Nix! The pixie flew at Sesame's throat and tugged at her locket.

"My master Zorgan, the magician, must have this!" demanded Nix.

"No way!" yelled Sesame, wrestling the pixie with her free hand. In the other she gripped the lantern charm.

BONG . . .

Gemma and Liz disappeared through a magical silvery mist into the sphere, now hovering and ready to go. But Maddy heard Sesame's shout; she was horrified to see Nix attacking Sesame and yanking at her locket. There wasn't a second to lose, so Maddy grabbed Sesame's arm.

"We have to go NOW!" she shouted urgently.

BONG!

With one last effort Sesame pushed Nix away, as Maddy dragged her through the mist, and the girls felt the balloon lift off . . .

". . . lights out now," Lossy was saying, as the girls found themselves back in Sesame's room. Everything was exactly as they'd left it, sleeping bags ready and the Crystal Chix still playing.

In a daze, Sesame felt for her locket. It was still there. She blinked. It seemed only *seconds* ago she'd been fighting off that horrid pixie! It's weird, she thought. The pixie said Zorgan wants my necklace. I wonder why?

After Lossy had said goodnight and closed the door, Sesame sat on her bed and opened her jewellery box. The Charmseekers took it in turns to hold the silver lantern to look at it, before Sesame placed it carefully with the other charms.

"It's lucky we fell down that pit," said Liz, snuggling into her sleepin -bag. "We might never have found it, if we hadn't."

Gemma gave a rueful smile, recalling how dark and cold it had been down there.

"Hmm," she said. "So, you think we should thank the *gribblers* for finding it!"

And they all laughed as Sesame switched off the light.

Ten

The Silversmith sighs with relief, as another magic candle flickers and dies. Ah, it is the lantern that has been found, for she sees it is the candle that bears its name that has gone out. "Six charms safe, seven more to find," she says aloud.

Despite her joy at knowing six charms are with Sesame in the Outworld, she senses her Seeker is in great danger. More so now than ever before!

Something has happened – something has changed that may cause her Charmseeker pain at some time in the future. Nevertheless, she knows Sesame will find the courage to continue her quest until all the charms are found.

Morbrecia and Zorgan are the main cause of her concern, and she fears Zorgan in particular may be plotting to harm Sesame, or put her under a spell. The very thought of the consequences were *that* to happen, sends a shiver down her spine, like a trickle of melted ice . . .

The Silversmith's quicksilver thoughts suddenly dart to The Ice Country in the north. Ever since the charm bracelet was stolen, the climate on Karisma has changed. She has heard the ice in that beautiful region is melting fast!

But that is another story. It must be told another day!

Acknowledgments

I owe a debt of gratitude to all those who have worked behind the scenes at Orion Children's Books and beyond to bring the *Charmseekers* books and their thirteen delightful charms to you. Since it would take more space than this edition allows to mention individuals by name, suffice it to say that I'm hugely grateful to my publishers and everyone involved with the publication of this series. In particular, my special thanks go to: my publisher, Fiona Kennedy, for her faith in believing I could write way beyond my own expectations. Her creative, tactful and skilful editing kept Sesame Brown on the right track and helped me to write a better story; my agent, Rosemary Sandberg; Jenny Glencross and Jane Hughes (Editorial); Alex Nicholas and Helen Speedy (Rights) Loulou Clark and Helen Ewing (Design); Clare Hennessy (Production); Jessica Killingley and Jo Dawson (Marketing); Pandora White (Orion Audio Books); Imogen Adams (Website designer – www.hammerinheels.com); Neil Pymer, the *real* Spinner Shindigs, for kind permission to use his name; and last, but by no means least, a million thanks go to my husband Tom for his inexhaustible patience, critical appraisal and support along the way.

Georgie Adams